D0343812

For Phil
~*JW*

For Pamela & Robin
~*GR*

EAST SUSSEX

V	W&S	INV No.	0199079
SHELF MARK			
COPY No.			
BRN			
DATE 25/7/00	LOC	LOC	LOC	LOC	LOC	LOC

COUNTY LIBRARY

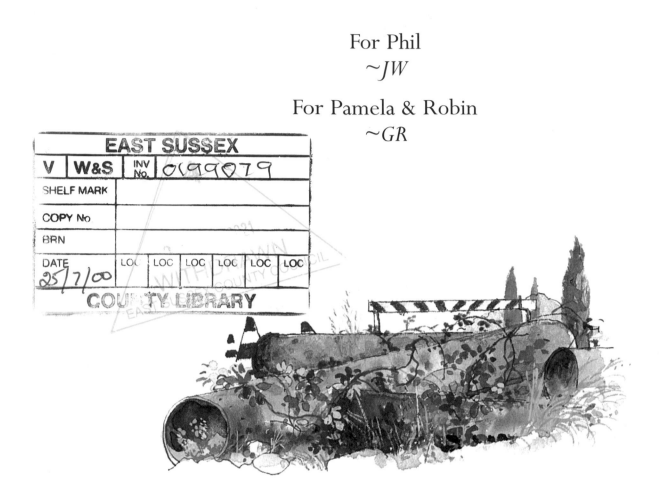

LITTLE TIGER PRESS
An imprint of Magi Publications
1 The Coda Centre, 189 Munster Road, London SW6 6AW
First published in Great Britain 2000
Text © 2000 Judy Waite
Illustrations © 2000 Gavin Rowe
Judy Waite and Gavin Rowe have asserted their rights
to be identified as the author and illustrator of this work
under the Copyright, Designs and Patents Act, 1988.
Printed in Belgium by Proost NV, Turnhout
All rights reserved • ISBN 1 85430 638 3
1 3 5 7 9 10 8 6 4 2

THE *Stray Kitten*

BY JUDY WAITE
ILLUSTRATED BY GAVIN ROWE

LITTLE TIGER PRESS
London

He was just a scrap of a kitten,
living amongst a muddle of old
pipes and brambles at the edge of the road.
It was a rough, hard life, and he was always
hungry.
Sometimes he hunted insects or small
creatures. Sometimes he found bits of food
tossed lazily away by the people that wandered
past. But he didn't pounce on the food.
He circled it slowly.

He had learnt to be watchful.

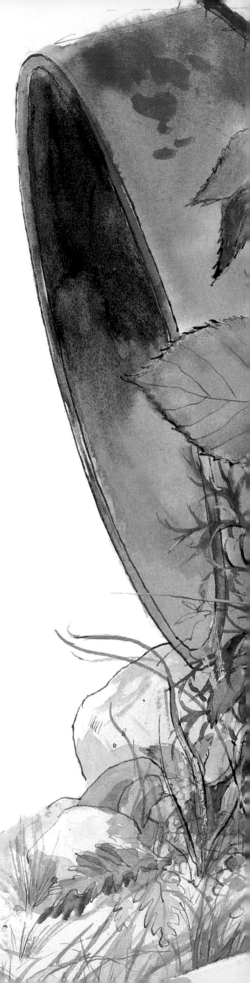

One day some children came by. They were fun at first,
but after a while the kitten grew tired and crept
inside the pipes.
The children shouted and wiggled sticks at him, but he
didn't come out again. At last they got bored and went
away. All except the smallest boy. He sat by the pipes,
calling softly. But the kitten didn't move or make a sound.

He had learnt to be quiet.

Hunger always gnawed at the kitten, and as he grew bigger, so it grew worse.
From the distance came a waft of sweet, rich smells and he slunk towards it down the dusty evening streets. He kept to the shadows, away from the roar of cars and the sudden barking of dogs on chains.

He had learnt to be careful.

The place of rich, sweet smells was lit with a hundred tiny lights. The kitten crept softly amongst the forest of chairs and tables.

The smells drove him crazy but he slid into the shadowed space between tubs of summer flowers and waited. His sharp green eyes watched carefully. His tail twitched, and his whiskers quivered, but he stayed hidden.

He had learnt to be patient.

When the food was thrown there was a rush of cats. The kitten rushed with them and a small boy tossed him scraps of fish. The sweet taste sang in his mouth.

The other cats were jealous. They arched and hissed, they spat and clawed. But the kitten arched and clawed back.

He had learnt how to fight.

After that, the kitten followed the smells every
night, growing bigger and stronger on the
scraps of people's meals. He was not a kitten any
more.

But then there came a night when there were no
people. Instead, the wind whipped the cloths from
the tables, and the sea flung angrily against the shore.
The young cat sat for a long time, watching the door
from where the food had been carried.

He had learnt to be hopeful.

The young cat's stomach twisted from thoughts
of food. In desperation, he leapt on to the
window ledge, calling loudly to the people inside.
Suddenly the door was flung
open and a shouting
woman hurled out a
bowl of cold water.
He fled in panic.
He would not cry
by windows again.

*He had learnt
to be wise.*

As the days passed, hunger tore at the cat. At night he sloped through wind-torn gardens, clawing at the bags of rubbish. He would eat anything, however bad it smelt, however foul it tasted.

But, even as he scratched and scrabbled in his desperate
search, he was always ready to run from danger.

He had learnt to be quick.

The weather grew worse. Most of the houses were
empty and shuttered. No rich, sweet smells ever
filled the air. No bags of rubbish appeared in the gardens.
And amongst the rain-lashed grass and brambles, no small
creatures or insects stirred.
The cat lay, thin and cold, inside the damp, rusting pipes
and hardly moved. He was weak and tired.

He had learnt not to care.

One morning, very early, the cat was woken by an angry rumble. He heard voices and shouting. The ground heaved and shook. Everywhere the air roared, and in terror he flattened himself against the rattling pipes. Something enormous was crashing down upon him. His fur rose and his eyes were wild.

He had learnt about fear.

Suddenly, someone was reaching for him. He was carried gently into a garden, past a window and through a door. He was too weak to struggle. At first he crept to a dark, low place and wouldn't come out.

But sweet, rich smells were drifting towards him. He sniffed the air, remembering. Then slowly, nervously, he moved towards the smells and began to eat.

He had learnt to be brave.

As the warm air slipped back into the days, the cat grew strong and healthy. Sometimes he lay in the garden, lazily watching the insects. Sometimes he caught the muddled smells of people and scraps and places with a hundred lights. But he never slunk through the shadows to find them. He was quiet enough to be petted. Patient enough to be cuddled. Brave enough to be stroked.

He had learnt to be loved.